World of Read

STAR WARS REBELS™

KANAN'S
JEDI TRAINING

ADAPTED BY ELIZABETH SCHAEFER

BASED ON THE EPISODE "PATH OF THE JEDI,"
WRITTEN BY CHARLES MURRAY

DISNEY

LUCASFILM
PRESS

LOS ANGELES • NEW YORK

Printed in the United States of America

First Edition, August 2015   10 9 8 7 6 5 4 3 2 1

Library of Congress Control Number: 2015934638

G658-7729-4-15170

ISBN 978-1-4847-0563-6

Visit the official *Star Wars* website at: www.starwars.com.

Meet Kanan.

Kanan is a Jedi.

He can use the Force.

The Force is an energy field.

It connects all living things.

The Force is strong with Kanan.

It can help him lift heavy things and jump very high.

The Force also helps Kanan sense if something is wrong.

As a Jedi, Kanan uses the Force to fight evil.

Once, there were many Jedi. But the evil Empire hunted them down.

But Kanan is not alone.

He fights the Empire with his rebel friends.

The rebels want everyone to be safe and free.

One of the other rebels can even use the Force.

His name is Ezra.

Kanan is training Ezra to be a Jedi, too.

Kanan has a lot to teach Ezra.

Jedi must learn how to fight with a lightsaber.

They must learn how to listen to the Force.

And they must learn to follow rules.

Ezra is not very good at following rules.

Kanan worries that he is not a good teacher.

One day, Kanan said Ezra was ready for his first big test.

They flew to Lothal, where there was an old Jedi temple.

Kanan told Ezra to find the temple.

"Let the Force guide you," Kanan said.

Ezra closed his eyes and listened to the Force.

The answer did not come right away.

Ezra let his doubts distract him. He was afraid that he would not find the temple.

"Trust yourself," Kanan told Ezra.

Finally, Ezra let his mind go blank. He let the Force speak to him.

It told him where to find the temple.

Ezra showed Kanan where to fly.

Soon they arrived at the old Jedi temple.

Together, Kanan and Ezra opened the big stone door.

Ezra and Kanan walked inside.

"In here, you'll have to face your worst fears," Kanan explained.

He hoped his teaching had been good enough to help Ezra.

Ezra walked into a maze of tunnels. He wasn't sure which way to turn.

Instead of using the Force, Ezra just picked one of the paths.

"Really? That's how you're choosing?"
Kanan said, following Ezra.

Ezra was hurt.

Kanan thought Ezra couldn't handle
the test alone.

Kanan didn't trust him.

"Come on," Kanan said. He ran down a path away from Ezra.

Ezra lost sight of Kanan.

Then he heard the hum of lightsabers and a cry of pain.

"Kanan?" Ezra called out.

Ezra ran and found Kanan fighting with the Inquisitor!

The Inquisitor was trained to hunt down and destroy Jedi.

He used the Force for evil.

The Inquisitor knocked Kanan to the ground. Then he turned to Ezra.

Ezra quickly picked up Kanan's lightsaber and tried to fight back.

But the lightsaber broke apart in his hands.

"Someone's not quite ready to become a Jedi," the Inquisitor said.

Ezra gave in to his fear. He left Kanan behind and tried to escape through a doorway.

But there was no ground on the other side! Ezra was falling!

Ezra landed in a familiar room.

It looked just like his bedroom on board the rebels' ship.

Then he heard his friends' voices.

"I don't think Ezra was ready," Hera said.

One by one, Sabine, Zeb, and Chopper agreed that Ezra must have failed.

Ezra felt sad. They didn't believe in him!

He had always been afraid that the rebels didn't really like him.

Then he stopped to think for a moment.

"This isn't you talking," he told the rebels. "I'm still back in the temple."

Ezra realized that everything he had seen was part of the test.

"This isn't real," Ezra said.

He ran from his friends and soon found himself back in the temple.

Maybe he had passed the test!

Ezra looked for Kanan.

But he found the Inquisitor instead.

Ezra had run from his fears twice now. This time, Ezra knew what to do.

"There's always a way out if I follow my training," he said.

He wasn't afraid of the Inquisitor's attack anymore.

When Ezra let go of his fear, the villain vanished.

Little lights appeared and led Ezra to a room deep in the temple.

There he found a small glowing
crystal.

Ezra took it and ran back to find
Kanan.

Kanan was happy that Ezra passed
the test.

Maybe Kanan was a good teacher
after all.

"What is this?" Ezra asked, holding
up the crystal.

"It's a lightsaber crystal," Kanan said.

With the crystal, Ezra could now make his own lightsaber.

It took weeks of work.

When Ezra was finished, he showed Kanan right away.

"Well, it's different," Kanan said.
"But that seems about right for you."

Ezra smiled. He turned on his
lightsaber for the first time.

Because of Kanan's training, Ezra was
one step closer to becoming a Jedi.